For Zenna

BLOOMSBURY CHILDREN'S BOOKS
Bloomsbury Publishing Inc., part of Bloomsbury Publishing Plc
1385 Broadway, New York, NY 10018

BLOOMSBURY, BLOOMSBURY CHILDREN'S BOOKS, and the Diana logo are trademarks of Bloomsbury Publishing Plc

First published in the United States of America in June 2019
by Bloomsbury Children's Books

Bloomsbury books may be purchased for business or promotional use. For information on bulk purchases please contact
Macmillan Corporate and Premium Sales Department at specialmarkets@macmillan.com

Library of Congress Cataloging-in-Publication Data
Names: Grant, Jacob, author, illustrator.
Title: Bear out there / by Jacob Grant.
Description: New York : Bloomsbury, 2019.
Summary: When Spider's kite gets stuck in a tree, he looks to his friend Bear for help, even though
Bear hesitates to leave his comfort zone.
Identifiers: LCCN 2018045171 (print) | LCCN 2018051306 (e-book)
ISBN 978-1-68119-745-6 (hardcover) • ISBN 978-1-68119-746-3 (e-book) • ISBN 978-1-68119-747-0 (e-PDF)
Subjects: | CYAC: Bears—Fiction. | Spiders—Fiction. | Friendship—Fiction.
Classification: LCC PZ7.G7667574 Bd 2019 (print) | LCC PZ7.G7667574 (e-book) | DDC [E]—dc23
LC record available at https://lccn.loc.gov/2018045171

Art made with charcoal, crayon, and ink and then colored digitally
Book design by Jacob Grant and John Candell
Typeset in Brandon Grotesque
Printed in China by Leo Paper Products, Heshan, Guangdong
2 4 6 8 10 9 7 5 3 1

To find out more about our authors and books visit www.bloomsbury.com and sign up for our newsletters.

Bear Out There

JACOB GRANT

BLOOMSBURY
CHILDREN'S BOOKS

NEW YORK LONDON OXFORD NEW DELHI SYDNEY

Spider had made a kite.
He was very excited to fly it out in the yard.

Spider loved the outdoors.
He liked the warm sun.
He liked the fresh breeze.
He liked the colorful plants all around.

The bugs were also nice.

His friend Bear did not agree.

"Who would want to go outside when there
are so many fun things to do inside?"

Bear had planned a tidy day at the house,
followed by a nice cup of tea in his cozy chair.

But plans have a way of changing.

"Spider, you are my friend, so I will help you find your kite," said Bear. "But you know I do not like the forest."

Bear did not like the filthy ground.
He did not like the itchy plants.
He did not like the pesky bugs all around.

Spider thought a search in the forest could
be fun. Then Bear began to grumble.

"Who would want to smell so many yucky weeds?" said Bear.

"Who would want to hear all this noisy twitter?"

"Who would ever want to see
such an unpleasant forest?"

The two friends walked on,
and still they could not find the kite.

Spider no longer thought the search
was much fun either.

The cold rain made Bear grumble
more than ever.

"What a mess!" he said. "Surely this
search cannot get any worse!"

But it could.

Bear did not grumble anymore.
Bear did not do anything at all.
Bear was done.

They had tried to find Spider's kite,
and they had failed.

"I am going home to my cozy chair
and a nice cup of tea," said Bear.

Bear paused for a long moment.
"Maybe we could look just a little farther."

Even if they could not find the kite, Spider was pleased to have his friend with him.

"We have not had much luck on our walk," said Bear. "But at least the rain is stopping."

When Spider and Bear looked up,
they saw more than clouds.

Back at home, the two friends patched up Spider's kite. And they even made something special for Bear.

"Now, who would want to relax with a nice cup of tea?" asked Bear.